D0464312

# Reggie

# Reggie

## Eve Bunting

## Illustrations by D. Brent Burkett

Cricket Books
Chicago

Library of Congress Cataloging-in-Publication Data

Bunting, Eve.

  Reggie / Eve Bunting ; illustrations by D. Brent Burkett.—1st ed.

    p. cm.

  Summary: Eight-year-old Alex is determined to keep the toy mouse he finds tied to a balloon, even after posters appear asking for its return, but when his dog Patch disappears, Alex discovers what it is like to lose something you love more than anything.

  ISBN-13: 978-0-8126-2746-6

  ISBN-10: 0-8126-2746-6

[1. Lost and found possessions—Fiction. 2. Dogs—Fiction.] I. Burkett, D. Brent, ill. II. Title.

  PZ7.B91527Reg 2006

  [E]—dc22

                 2006012065

For Anna and Pony Boy
—E. B.

For Ashley, Kelsey, and Ian
—D. B. B.

I was walking along the sidewalk with my dog, Patch, when the balloon came floating down. It bobbed and bobbled in front of me.

Patch began to bark and tug hard on his leash.

"O.K., Patch. Relax!" I told him. "It's just a balloon." But then I saw that there was something tied to the string, something holding the balloon down. I took another step. It was something very small, gray, and red.

I bent down to look closer, and oh my gosh! It was a mouse, dressed in a red vest. I don't know why, but the minute I saw that little mouse I was crazy about him. I had a sudden flash of a faraway memory that I couldn't catch hold of.

Patch was going bonkers, trying to get to him. I reined my dog in tight. "Quit it!" I growled.

The mouse wasn't moving. Was he dead? My heart almost stopped beating.

And then I realized. Of course it wasn't a real mouse. Whoever heard of a real mouse dressed in a red vest? It was just a stuffed toy.

I was afraid it might drift away again, so I grabbed for the string while Patch whimpered and pleaded to find out what was going on.

I held the string with its dangle of mouse well away from him.

"If I let go of you while I loosen this mouse, you could do something stupid," I told Patch. "Sorry, but I'll have to tie you up for a minute."

I looped the string to my belt so the balloon wouldn't float away, then wound Patch's leash round and round the trunk of the magnolia tree by the sidewalk. I tied the knot tight. My dog is clever. He can free himself from almost anything. He can even open doors and gates. My mom says we should have called him Houdini.

He gave me sorrowful looks as I pulled on the knot. Patch always tells me what he thinks.

I patted his head. "Sorry, Pup. I won't be long."

The little mouse had the string twisted around his waist. It wasn't even tied, but it was in a tangle, which was why it hadn't come loose. I used my teeth to unravel it, and all the time Patch whimpered and whined and pulled on his leash.

I held the mouse and let the string go. There was so little air left in the balloon that it skittered along, just inches above the sidewalk.

The mouse lay in my hand. He was the all-time coolest mouse I had ever seen, with his black button eyes and feathery whiskers and that little red vest. I let his tail dangle between my fingers.

"You are the all-time coolest mouse I've ever seen," I told him.

But the way I felt about him was more than that. It was like a tugging inside of me.

It was very strange.

Patch was going crazy, so I untied him and started for home. All the way there he jumped and leaped, trying to get my mouse. But I reminded him to relax and that he wouldn't want to eat this kind of mouse, anyway.

When we got home, Mom was in the living room, playing "Für Elise" again on the piano. Mom teaches sixth grade, and she started taking piano lessons at the beginning of summer vacation. I swear, if she doesn't learn to play something besides "Für Elise" soon, I'll have to leave home. "Für Elise" and scales.

"Look what I found," I said.

"Good heavens, Alex!" She peered down at my hand. "A mouse in a vest."

I explained about the balloon, rubbing my mouse's fat stomach under his vest as I talked.

I held him up and sniffed him. He smelled of stuffed toy and something sweet, like cotton candy.

That was the wrong smell.

I scratched my head. What kind of smell was I expecting?

"Who would float away a little mouse like this?" I asked Mom, hoping she hadn't noticed the sniffing business. Goofy for sure!

Mom shrugged. "Beats me. The balloon was probably filled with helium and was airborne for a while. Then the gas slowly escaped because rubber is permeable, so eventually the weight of the mouse and the laws of gravity brought it down. You know about gravity and Sir Isaac Newton, don't you, Alex? The gravitational force between two masses is inversely proportionate to the square root of the distance between them. You know about the apple?"

"I do," I said quickly. You have to stop Mom fast if you're going to stop her at all. In another second she'd be asking if I knew what "inversely whatever-it-was" meant. Even on summer vacation, Mom can't help spreading knowledge wherever she can. Which usually means to me. She says it's the teacher in her. I'm only in the third grade, but she's been talking to me like that all my life.

When Dad came in from the office, I told the story all over again.

"Gravity brought him down," I explained.

Dad nodded. "He's a good-looking mouse. That vest is exactly like the one my Scottish uncle, Reggie McAdoo, used to wear when he played golf."

I grinned. "All right! Reggie."

"I guess you'd better try to find whoever lost him," Mom said.

Was she kidding? As far as I was concerned, whoever lost him deserved to lose him.

Reggie was mine.

Chapter 2

That night I secretly made a bed for Reggie in the little box that had once held my swimming medal. I put a handkerchief that I borrowed from Dad's drawer in the box for Reggie to lie on and another one, folded, for his pillow.

Patch watched me with interest.

Once I caught him giving me a disgusted look. I'm really glad he can't blab, being a dog. Except to other dogs. I wouldn't want anyone, not even Mom or Dad, to know how silly I was with Reggie. How when I looked at him I went all mushy

inside, like I was full of warm tapioca. I mean, I laughed like a hyena last Christmas when my little cousin, Tiffany, made a bed in a shoebox for her two Beanie Babies. And here I was, eight years old, and a guy.

I put Reggie in his bed in the drawer of my nightstand so Mom and Dad wouldn't see him when they came to say good night. But as soon as they left, I took him out again and put him by my pillow.

Patch, as usual, lay on my feet on top of the covers.

"Good night, Patchie Pie," I told him. "Sweet doggy dreams. Don't you try to get at Reggie while I'm asleep, because I'll know if you do and you'll be in big trouble. O.K.?"

Patch sighed.

In the morning I got dressed and slipped Reggie back in the drawer.

"You can have another nap," I told him.

Patch and I went downstairs.

Mom was in the kitchen reading the *Pasadena Star-News.* Dad had already left for work.

I poured myself some Honey Stars.

"Listen to this," Mom said. "They've discovered that chewing gum burns off calories. Imagine that! I hope that doesn't mean I'll have to let my students chew gum all day long."

"Maybe they'll be able to do away with P.E.," I suggested. "Have gum-chewing classes instead."

"Chewing for one hour burns off eleven calories," Mom said thoughtfully.

I jumped up. "Interesting," I muttered.

I know the danger signs. In a minute she'd be asking me to do the math. "If you burn off eleven calories in one hour, how many could you burn off in a day, a month, given that the month has 31 days? Given that you slept for eight hours each night and chewed gum for sixteen?"

"I'm going to ride my bike over to Brian's and tell him about Reggie," I announced. "O.K.?"

"Sure," she said. I think she was busy doing the math herself.

Brian is my best buddy, who lives on the next block. I never take Patch over to his house, though, because he has a mean old fat cat, and that cat and Patchie are mortal enemies.

I was just swinging around the corner onto Oakland, where Brian lives, when I spotted a white notice taped on the lamppost. I slowed and stopped, balancing one foot on the curb. It said:

LOST ONE MOUSE
DRESSED IN RED VEST
$5 REWARD $5
RETURN TO 365
CRAIG AVENUE

Oh-oh! Craig Avenue. That was just three streets away from my house. Newton's law of gravity had worked fast.

I read the notice again. Five dollars reward. That was how much this person thought of Reggie. That was how much it was worth to get him back.

Well, he was worth a heck of a lot more than that to me. I thought of him, and I was filled with warm tapioca again.

My mind slithered around. Who knew I'd found him? Only Patch, who wouldn't tell, and my mom and dad. Fortunately, I hadn't told Brian yet.

The fewer people who knew, the better.

But if Mom and Dad saw this notice, they'd definitely want me to take Reggie back. And the chance of them seeing the notice was pretty good. Driving in a car, you might miss it. But they often took Patch for a night walk. And the lamppost was right there.

I looked up and down my street. Then I looked along Oakland toward Brian's house. There was nobody except Mrs. Escondito in her blue bathrobe, out watering her roses.

Quick as a flash I ripped the notice off the pole and jammed it in the back pocket of my shorts.

No way were they going to get Reggie back.

Chapter 3

I didn't want to go to Brian's now. I needed time. A thought cold as a snake wriggled into my head. What if there were other missing-mouse posters? Would anyone put up just one? There had to be more.

I cycled back the way I'd come.

Mrs. Escondito waved her garden hose at me. The curve of water made a rainbow in the morning sun.

"Wait up, Alex," she called, screwing the nozzle so the water trickled to a stop.

I waited. Had she seen me peel that poster off the lamppost? She couldn't have. Her back had been to me all the time. I was sweating a little, and it wasn't even warm yet.

She came across to me. Her blue bathrobe had little yellow ducks printed all over it.

"What's on the flier?" she asked, nodding toward the corner.

"Ah-ah-what flier?" I couldn't help it. One of my hands slid around to cover my back pocket. My bike wobbled, and maybe my knees, too.

Mrs. Escondito peered around me at the lamppost. "Where did it go? It was there a minute ago."

"Where did what go?"

Was that a suspicious look she was giving me? Or just a puzzled one?

"Don't be dense, Alex. I'm talking about that flier. A kid about your age came by and stuck it up on the lamppost an hour or so ago. I was wondering what it was all about."

I counted the ducks on her sleeve so I wouldn't have to look her in the eyes and said, "Don't ask me."

"Ah well," she said. "It must have fallen off. Probably one of those nasty garage sale announcements, people selling all their junk. And mis-guided people buying it, too."

I nodded.

She turned the nozzle on her hose, and water shot again, which I guessed was my signal to leave.

I was happy to go.

But she'd remember me being there, right after the crime. She'd be a witness. She'd have no trouble picking me out of a lineup.

I pedaled furiously back along my street, past our house where piano notes drifted like birds through our open living room window.

Down at the corner of Bonnie, I saw something white and square on the lamppost. Oh no. Oh yes. From here it looked like the twin of the notice I had in my back pocket.

A woman pushing a stroller had stopped to read it. She glanced at me over her shoulder. "Someone's lost a mouse. I'd be happy to give him the one that's leaving his little you-know-whats behind my refrigerator."

I smiled a weak smile and pedaled on. I couldn't go round the whole neighborhood swiping these things. I'd be caught for sure. The next street was Craig. No way was I going there!

I turned the corner onto Brian's street, making sure to give the left turn signal the way Dad showed me.

Even though there wasn't a car or a bike or a person on the street. Dad and Mom are strict about bicycle safety. Right away I spotted another flier, taped to the tree in front of his house. Bad news! That kid had covered the whole neighborhood. Would I dare take this one? And then I saw Brian. He was shooting baskets into the net above his garage door. Brian's good, and he has a theory that if he practices two hours every day he'll turn into Shaq O'Neal. He was twisting and hopping and making shots behind his back and through his legs. When he saw me, he beamed. "Watch this!" His behind-the-back shot dropped right into the net.

"Outrageous!" I said. And it was. Maybe his theory is 100 percent right and he'll play for the Lakers someday,

and as his best friend I'll have season court seats. "Keep practicing," I told him.

"What's happening?" he asked, then nodded at the poster. "See this thing about the mouse?"

"Yeah."

"You know what? Jehosephat could find this mouse in a lick split."

Jehosephat is Brian's big fat mean old cat.

"Jehosephat is a bloodhound where mice are concerned." He balanced the ball on his toe, then kicked it up into his hands.

"Cool," I told him.

Brian nodded. "Thanks. Anyway, I could take Jehosephat down to that house, give him a whiff of something that belonged to the mouse, and he'd be on the trail in a nanosecond. Five bucks! We could go straight to

31 Flavors and get two chocolate cherry pistachio sundaes with double sprinkles." He grinned at me happily. "Is that a plan?"

"This isn't a real mouse, you know," I told him. "It's just a virtual mouse. Stuffed."

Brian's grin fizzled. "No kidding."

"Did you ever see a real mouse wearing a vest?"

"Well, they should have put that on the flier, then," Brian said. "That was misleading."

But Brian never stays bummed out for long. "Want to go to the park?" he asked. "I told Danny Jackson and the other guys we'd be up for a game of baseball."

I wasn't sure. I had too many worries right now to think about baseball.

"Aw, c'mon," Brian urged. "What else do you have to do?"

"Plenty. But I don't know what," I said. "O.K., I suppose. But I'll have to go home first and get my mitt and . . ." I almost said, get rid of this poster that's burning a hole in my pocket. But I didn't, of course.

"Hold up and I'll come with you." Brian dropped the basketball and ran across to the porch, where his mitt lay on the wicker rocker. He picked it up. "I'll get my bike."

I stood there, waiting for him, and I suddenly realized something. If he came to my house, my mom would probably say something about Reggie. About how I'd found him. And for sure then Brian would mention the poster. Mom would be shocked.

She'd tell me that I had to go, this very minute, and take that mouse back to the boy who obviously wanted him in the worst way.

It looked like I'd have to keep Mom and Dad away from those fliers.

And away from Brian, too.

How complicated could dishonesty be? It was like juggling 31 balls at the same time.

This would never work.

There was only one thing I could do, and I'd have to do it fast.

Chapter 4

I didn't want to confess to Brian. But it was that or never let him come to my house again. Because if he did, he and Mom would be sure to discuss this and that, and the mouse and the poster would both come up. I didn't want to think about what would happen next.

Jehosephat was watching and listening on the porch steps. He's a black-and-gray-striped cat and he has a face like a bad-tempered Pekingese. But Brian and his little sisters love him. I didn't mind Jehosephat hearing because he was like Patch. He'd never tell.

When Brian came back with his bike, I said, "First, you have to give the 'may my arms fall off' promise."

"I promise," he said, chopping at each arm in turn with his other hand.

"Sacred?" I asked.

"Sacred."

I told him about Reggie.

He stared at me. "You stole the mouse?"

"No, I didn't. He came floating down from the sky. From heaven almost. Honestly."

Brian had this funny look on his face.

I tried not to whine. "He came to me. I didn't go out and steal him. You can ask Patch," I added quickly.

"But you're stealing him now," Brian said. "Because now you know who he belongs to. You have to give him back."

"Uh-uh," I said. "He's mine. Finders keepers."

I thought of Reggie's little button eyes and feathery whiskers, and that feeling came over me again. That strange, squishy feeling that I couldn't begin to understand.

"What do you want a mouse for?" Brian asked. "It's not even a live mouse that you could teach to do tricks."

He chewed on an edge of his mitt and watched me over the top of it.

"I dunno," I said. "It's just . . . I don't know. His name's Reggie. Reggie mouse."

"Whatever. You stole him."

"Did not." Jehosephat had come over, deeply interested, and Brian picked him up. They both glowered at me.

"Forget you, Brian!" I got on my bike and started pedaling like mad.

"Where is this dumb mouse?" he shouted at my back, putting down the cat. He grabbed his bike and pedaled behind me.

"Sh!" I looked nervously around. "He's at home."

"Are you going to show me?"

I shrugged. "If you want."

We were at the corner of Craig. Suddenly Brian whizzed past me.

Where was he going? Was he going to tell the mouse guy?

"If you go blab to him, I'll never speak to you again. You won't even be my friend." It flashed through my mind that if he wasn't my friend, I'd never get those front-row seats at the Lakers games. But even so.

"I just want to see where he lives," Brian shouted over his shoulder.

"What for?"

He pretended not to hear.

340, 342. There it was. 365.

"It's the house that was just sold," Brian said.

"Let's go," I began, and stopped.

There was a kid in the front yard, a kid in shorts and a red T-shirt and—more bad news. What was that he had in his hand? A wad of fliers, just like the one I'd taken, the one heating up my back pocket.

"Hi," the kid called.

And what was up with Brian? He was stopping. "What you got there?" he asked.

"The sacred promise," I said loudly. "Don't forget the sacred promise."

"These are posters," the guy said. "I'm putting them up all over."

"Oh, about your mouse," Brian said.

I gave him a dirty look, let go of one handlebar, and chopped at my arm.

The boy walked toward us. "Yeah, the mouse. You haven't seen him, have you?" I wished he didn't look so hopeful all of a sudden.

"I haven't seen him," Brian said. "I've just heard about him."

I was praying the guy wouldn't ask me.

"And I saw one of your posters," Brian added. "What's your name?"

"Ira."

"I'm Brian and . . . ," he jerked a thumb, "this is Alex."

"Well, I hope somebody finds that mouse," Ira said. "He belongs to my little sister, Sally. She's crying and moping all round the house. It's pretty sad. Sally loves that silly mouse more than anything."

Brian flicked me a look and then said, "I know what you mean. My little sister Dodo lost her canary bird once, and it was sob city till she found him."

For some reason they were both looking hard at me. Or maybe not!

I coughed. "He sounds like a state-of-the-art mouse, all right. I mean, with that vest and all." My voice sounded really sympathetic, which was bogus. I was thinking, if his sister was so careless, well, she deserved to lose Reggie, that was all.

"Couldn't she get another stuffed mouse the same?" Brian asked.

"Uh-uh," said Ira. "To her this is a one-of-a-kind mouse. My dad brought him to her from Switzerland. She accepts no substitutes. She was giving him a ride on a balloon when he floated away. Can you believe that? Now she's offering this five-dollar reward, which is all the money she's got. She's been saving for a tiara."

"What's a tiara?" I asked.

"It's a crown made of cardboard and fake diamonds," Brian said. "Girls use them when they play fairy princess."

"Or ballerina," Ira said.

"Or Cinderella."

Ira nodded. "That, too."

Sometimes I feel really out of it, not having a sister with a tiara. Mostly I just feel lucky.

And then the screen door opened, and this little girl came out.

She wasn't the kind of kid you'd see in a TV commercial or in an ad for Honey Stars cereal. She was kind of pudgy and she had glasses and straight hair and her face had a million freckles. She'd painted her fingernails black. They looked like squashed blackberries.

I thought maybe she was in mourning.

She walked right over to me.

Uh-oh. I began to squirm.

"Did you bring back my mouse?" she asked.

Chapter 5

I took a step backward.

"Of course he didn't bring back your mouse." Ira's voice was gentle. "Sally asks everyone who comes in the yard," he explained to me. "She asked the man who came to turn on the electricity, the phone man, the gardener, makes no difference to Sally."

"I'm sorry," I told her. "I didn't bring back your mouse." And right then, I was sorry.

She trailed back into the house.

"Alex? Alex?" Brian's voice was urgent. More than anything, he wanted me to tell her I would bring Reggie back, even if I didn't have him with me right now.

I nodded toward the posters Ira held. "How many of those are you putting up?"

"Seventeen," he said. "I already did eight."

"That's a lot of posters," I said weakly.

He held them up. "Want to help me?"

Brian jumped off his bike. "Sure," he said.

I coughed. "What about the game, Brian? Don't forget we're going to the park. We're supposed to meet the others there." I was thinking, HE'S going to help put up posters . . . what a traitor! He's supposed to be my friend.

"Oh, O.K.," Brian said. "Want to come play baseball instead, Ira?"

"How about tomorrow? Could I come then? Maybe Mouser will have turned up, and I won't feel like I have to keep searching for him." He looked apologetic. "It's just . . . Sally's so unhappy."

"Mouser? Is that his name?" I asked nervously.

Ira grinned. "Yeah. Dumb name!"

"There's a game going on most days in Grant Park," Brian told him. "That's just a couple of blocks away. We'll come get you."

I tugged at his arm. "C'mon, Brian. We gotta go."

I started off, and Brian trailed behind me. "I hope you feel like a jerk," he shouted at my back.

I put my head down almost over

my handlebars and raced. I couldn't outride him, though. His voice griped away. "What's the matter with you, anyway? All this over a mouse."

I turned around. "Sh!"

But I was thinking, what *is* the matter with me? I pictured myself going back to my room, lifting Reggie, bringing him back to the little girl with the three million freckles and the blackberry nails. She'd be so stoked. But then I pictured the empty box where Reggie had been, and this awful loneliness came upon me. What was the matter with me? Brian was right. All this over a mouse.

We jumped off our bikes in my driveway. "And don't you forget the promise," I said, putting my face close to Brian's. "I'll make the mouse decision. Just remember, it will be really hard to be like Shaq if your arms have fallen off."

Brian threw his bike down on the grass.

"If there's a crime and you know it and you keep quiet, then you're an accomplice," he muttered. "And you shouldn't keep that quiet because . . ."

"What did you say?" I asked sharply.

"Nothing."

But I'd heard.

We stamped up onto the porch. Mom was blissfully playing "Für Elise," trilling her fingers over the keys, her arms pumping. Patch lay at her feet. "Your mom sure loves that tune," Brian said.

I nodded grimly.

"Hi, guys! Want some food?" Mom asked, not missing a note. She always asks that. She's a really cool mom. I didn't want to think what she'd say if she knew all that was going on over Reggie.

"Mrs. Carson, you sure play good," Brian said. "You're just about as good as Mozart."

Mom swung around and beamed at us. "Brian! You are the joy of my heart. Do you know about Mozart? He composed five piano pieces when he was only four years old."

"No kidding," Brian said. "And didn't he go deaf?"

"That was Beethoven." Mom flexed her fingers, doing her finger exercises. She's really serious about this piano stuff. "Beethoven, now . . . ," she began.

"We've got to go, Mom," I said quickly. I've told Brian a hundred times not to get Mom started, but he always shrugs and says, "So what? It's interesting."

"Have you seen Reggie yet?" Mom asked Brian. "He's a pretty cute mouse."

"Alex told me. He's going to show me now."

I imagined how this would have gone down if I hadn't leveled with Brian.

"What cute mouse?" Brian would have asked. "You mean Alex has this poster mouse?" Et cetera, et cetera.

It was smart of me to have told him.

We went upstairs, Patch leaping along behind us.

I opened the drawer of my night-stand, and there was Reggie, snug in his soft bed. I felt this rush of relief, which was dumb. Where else would he be? Did I think this was *The X-Files* or something and he'd come alive while I was gone and skedaddled away?

"He is cute, all right," Brian said. "Is it O.K. if I pick him up?"

"Sure."

He lifted Reggie out of his box, and Patch jumped up, tongue lolling, to snuff and snuffle.

"Quit," I told him sharply, pushing him away. "Don't you dare touch Reggie." I'd pushed harder than I meant to, and Patch's claws skidded across my wooden floor. The bedside mat skidded along beneath him.

"Sorry," I muttered, not looking at Patch, wiping a small fleck of his spit off Reggie.

"Patch was only sniffing, man," Brian said. "Dogs sniff. Cats, too. Jehosephat is the world's loudest sniffer. *Snurf, snurf, snurf.*" He gave me a loud example of Jehosephat's talent, then bent over Reggie.

Patch sat straight up on his crumpled mat and watched me warily.

I went across to him and tried to rub behind his ears. "Sorry, fellow," I whispered. "I hate it that I did that!"

Patch pulled his head away.

I came back over to Brian. "See what I mean?" I asked. "This is a supercool mouse. No way am I going to give him back. Ira's little sister lost him, and that's her hard luck." My voice sounded pleading, even to myself. More than anything, I wanted Brian to say, "No kidding! I wouldn't give him up either, if I found him." But he didn't say a thing, just gave Reggie back to me.

I put my little mouse in the box while he and Patch watched. Piano scales wafted lightly up the stairs. I slid the box back in my nightstand drawer, wishing I could stop thinking about the little kid's freckled face.

"I don't see what good he is if you have to keep him hidden away," Brian said. "You can't take him outside and show him to the other guys. I mean, what good is he if you have to keep him locked up?" He plunked down on my bed. "It's like my aunt Martha," he said. "She has this great ring with a humongous ruby or something. It's worth a ton of money. She keeps it in a safety-deposit box. What fun is that?"

"The drawer is not locked, if you must know. I lost the key. I would lock it if I could."

Brian sniffed. "Nobody's going to steal him." He turned his face away from me and added, "Even if you did."

I felt my face get hot. "Now, wait a second . . . ," I began.

Brian stared at me hard. "You

know what? I don't even like you anymore. I don't want to have you as a friend."

He stomped out and slammed the door behind him.

Chapter 6

So what? I muttered to myself. So Brian's not my friend anymore and he doesn't even like me. So what?

But it was a big what. Brian and I had been mad at each other before, but this was different. This time he'd been serious. Grown-up serious.

I chewed on my fingernails. The only thing that would fix this for me was to give Reggie back. But . . . but I couldn't.

Was there any way to keep him and still have Brian be my friend? Because . . . because I'd miss Brian an awful lot.

I chewed at my fingernails some more.

And then I had an idea that came like a zag of lightning.

Of course! I'd pay for Reggie. That would make it legal. Brian would forgive me, and all would be well.

In the drawer with Reggie was my bankbook. I looked at my latest balance. $48.35. O.K.! I put the book in my top pocket, then had a short conversation with my mouse. I told him I was working on how to bring him out of the drawer and into the world, and maybe I'd figured out a way. Then I went downstairs.

Mom was making little meatballs to simmer in the spaghetti sauce for dinner. The kitchen smelled wonderful. She had on one of her old LPs, records that are as big as dinner plates.

The record was of someone called Liberace who played piano back in my grandmother's day. Mom says he always played with a candelabrum on top of his piano, day and night, and he had a humongous smile that looked like piano keys, the white ones only. He sounded weird, but she said he was a really nice man and a great pianist, too.

Patch had come downstairs behind me. He set himself close to Mom.

I patted my leg and held out a dog biscuit. "Here, Patch."

He didn't come.

When I brought the biscuit over and said, "Here, doggy," he took it without looking at me. Certainly he took it. Patch is no dummy.

"What did you do to offend him?" Mom asked, humming along with Mr. Liberace.

"Oh, he's just pouty," I said. Patch stuck up his nose to show me I'd offended him even more.

"I'm going out for a while," I told Mom.

"Where did Brian go?"

"He had a softball game. I didn't feel like playing." I heard his voice saying, "I don't even like you anymore. I don't want to have you as a friend." I squeezed my ears tight so I wouldn't have to listen.

"Any chance of a meatball sample?" I asked Mom, and she fished one out and gave it to me on a fork. She took one out for Patch, too, and blew on it before she set it in his dish.

I got my bike, wheeled up to the Bank America two blocks from my house, and got in line. My favorite teller, Miss Chickweed, was there, and I waited for her. When I first saw her behind the counter, I thought she must be Miss Chick Weed, but I discovered she is Miss Elaine Chickweed and she is beautiful. Curly hair and everything. She has a million-dollar smile, which is good for someone who works in a bank. It's probably like Mr. Liberace's, only smaller.

"Making a deposit?" she asked.

"I'm taking it all out," I told her.

"Better leave a dollar so you can come back and visit," she suggested, so I did.

At home, I went in my room, put the $47.35 in an envelope, and carefully printed on lined paper:

I FOUND MOUSER AND I WANT
TO KEEP HIM. HERE IS SOME

MONEY SO YOU CAN BUY A
TIARA INSTEAD. IF THIS IS O.K.
WITH YOU, HANG A RIBBON OR
SOMETHING ON THE TREE IN
YOUR YARD SO I'LL KNOW.
                    A FRIEND

I had to look up the spelling of the word *tiara* in the dictionary, a practice that Mom encourages.

"Tiara," it said. "A high, dome-shaped diadem worn by the pope." That couldn't be right. Then below that definition, I saw "A jeweled or profusely decorated ornament worn by women above the forehead." Bingo. I hoped the $47.35 would be enough, but it probably would since this one wasn't for the pope. She'd make the exchange for sure, and I'd be in the clear.

I folded the envelope into my back pocket.

Downstairs I took a look at the meatballs, waiting patiently in the sauce. I love Mom's spaghetti and meatballs. I love dinnertime. But first . . .

As usual when I headed for the door, Patch came cavorting, hoping for a walk or some ball-chasing in the yard. "Not this time," I told him, pushing him down. He gave me a dirty look, walked across the kitchen, and sat down with his back to me.

"Oh, you're really in his bad graces," Mom said.

"Get a life, dog," I told him. "I'll be back in five minutes," I told Mom.

I rode to 365 Craig. Ira had been busy, for sure. There were posters on every tree and lamppost in sight. I decided he'd take them down as soon as his little sister accepted my offer.

The blue station wagon I'd noticed before wasn't in the driveway, so I felt safe going up to the door and putting the letter in their mailbox. I glanced sideways at their oak tree. There was a nice low branch ready and waiting for a ribbon.

Riding home, I felt good. Little kids forget easily, I told myself. I'd heard that somewhere, most likely on the TV. Sally will probably like the tiara more than Mouser anyway. And she'll be so excited about going to buy it with real money that the mouse will be history. I imagined the big, wide smile on her freckly face under the jeweled or profusely decorated ornament that would be above her forehead.

It seemed that Reggie was more mine now. It was as if I'd bought him. And, hey, that's what I could say if Mom or Dad saw one of those posters. "Oh, since then I've paid for him." That wouldn't be a lie, would it? I felt lighter and happier. In a way, Reggie had dropped out of the sky for me, and the tiara had dropped out of the sky for the little kid.

But what if she didn't want to exchange? I wouldn't even think about that.

I whistled one of Mr. Liberace's tunes and decided to bring Reggie down to eat dinner with us . . . get him out of the box for a while.

At our corner lamppost, I saw Ira had been on the job again. Where I'd ripped off the other flier, he'd put up a new one. Oh well, tomorrow he'd probably take them all down. And by that time, Brian and I would for sure be friends again. Already I was missing him.

Chapter 7

Dad was coming home from work just as I wheeled into the driveway. I opened the gate for both of us, waited while he put the car in the garage, and latched it again behind us. We walked in the back door together.

Dad went straight to Mom and hugged and kissed her, which is very usual. They are always canoodling, as Mom calls it. I think parents canoodling is a good thing for kids to see. It's neat. My friend Steve Podley told me once that his parents never canoodle, which I think is sad.

"Where's Patch?" I asked Mom.

"He's out in the backyard, still pouting," she told me.

I went to the door. Patch was under the fig tree chewing on something old and juicy, probably the ancient tennis shoe that is his favorite chewable. He didn't even look up when I called. "Patchie Pudding Pal," I murmured, "don't be like this. Do I have to get down on my knees and apologize to you? I was mean, pushing you like that. I'm sorry."

He kept on chewing. I'd hurt his feelings, and he was going to give me a hard time.

"O.K., be that way," I said, pouty myself, and went upstairs to get Reggie.

"You are the mouse of the world," I told him, admiring again the neat way he fitted my hand. "And you know something? I paid a whole bunch of money for you. And you know something else? You're worth it."

Looking down at him, I had that drift of memory again that disappeared like smoke before I could catch it.

I went slowly back downstairs carrying Reggie.

"Mom?" I asked as I came into the kitchen. "Did I ever have a mouse like Reggie before? Once sometime? Way in the past?" I smoothed my finger over his fat little stomach that bulged under the red vest. "He's, you know, like an old friend that's come back."

Dad was slicing tomatoes on the cutting board, and he turned around. "What about Pony Boy?" he asked Mom.

Mom's eyes widened. "But Pony Boy wasn't a mouse. He was a little horse. And you couldn't possibly remember him, Alex. You were . . . what? Three years old."

"Pony Boy?" I repeated.

"He was just about the size of Reggie," Dad said. "Same color of velvety gray."

My heart started to thump.

Mom was holding the silverware, and she passed it to me. "You know what? Come to think of it, Pony Boy had a little red saddle blanket sewn onto his back."

"Aunt Sophie gave him to you when you were a baby," Dad said. "He was never out of your hand."

I began one-handed setting the silverware around the table.

Mom had that thinking-back look on her face. "You sucked on him till he was nearly bald. Poor Pony Boy. And when you got your first teeth, you gnawed on him." She smiled at Dad. "Remember how Alex wouldn't sleep without him? He'd have Pony Boy curled up in his fist, and we couldn't pry him out—unless you were sound asleep, Alex."

I looked down at my hand. Reggie was curled up in my fist, so tight that nobody could begin to pry him out.

"I guess I really liked that Pony Boy," I said.

"You loved him." Mom peered

into the pasta pot and gave the spaghetti a quick stir around. "Pony Boy was quite disgusting. He smelled of spit-up and strained spinach and sour formula, and that smell wouldn't come out no matter how often I sprayed him and sponged him. Which, as I said, had to be done while you were sleeping. You wouldn't let go of him when you were awake."

"What happened to him?" I asked. "Do we still have him?" And without thinking I lifted Reggie to my nose and took a long sniff. No Pony Boy smell there.

"We don't still have him," Mom said. "Poor Pony Boy came to an unfortunate end."

"How come?" I wasn't sure I wanted to know. Another flicker of memory, of tears, of sadness.

"We were on the ship going to Catalina Island. Dad was holding you, and you dropped poor Pony Boy over the side."

I stared at her. "On purpose?"

"Well, we were never sure. Maybe you wanted to see if he could swim. Or you wanted to cool him off. It was a really hot day. Or somehow he just dropped out of your clutches. What a catastrophe."

Looking down into a place far, far below. Looking for something in big blueness.

"You wailed and screamed. We almost had to put out a lifeboat to the rescue," Dad said. "And you know what? Pony Boy could swim. Or float, anyway. We saw him for a second, just a little dot in the ocean, and then he vanished."

"I had to stop your dad from diving in after him," Mom said, laughing.

Dad scratched his head. "It might have been worth it just to rescue him. You kept screeching, 'I want my Pony Boy. I want my Pony Boy.'"

Mom made a face at me. "And all that night you were so upset. We were in a lovely little hotel overlooking Avalon harbor. Do you remember?" she asked Dad.

Dad groaned. "How could I forget? The owners coming up in the night asking, 'Is there a way to keep your child quiet? We do have other guests.'

"As soon as we got home, which I might add we had to do a day early, we tried to find another Pony Boy, just like the one you lost. Of course, we couldn't."

"I would accept no substitute," I whispered.

"What?" Dad asked.

"Nothing," I said.

Mom poured a glass of milk and set it on the table at my place.

"Anyway," said Dad, "a new one wouldn't have smelled right. Or tasted right."

I stared at Dad. The fog in my mind was drifting away. It was because I'd lost Pony Boy that I'd grabbed on to Reggie. I knew it. Reggie had taken Pony Boy's space and filled it up. I couldn't let him go.

I wondered if I could sneak away after dinner and see if there was a ribbon on that tree.

I watched Dad wipe his hands on a paper towel and pour kibble into Patch's dish. He opened the back door and rattled the bowl. "Dinner-time," he called.

Usually Patch comes galumphing up the steps at the sound of that rattle. Tonight he didn't come.

"Dog!" Dad called. "You're going to love this. There's a meatball mixed in."

"He's still not speaking to me," I said. "I'll go get him."

Patch wasn't under the fig tree. I almost tripped over the old tennis shoe, which he'd abandoned.

"Patch?" I called, rattling the bowl. "You know what? I wasn't nice to you, but don't be mad." I figured he was probably crouched under the hedge, listening, so I lowered my voice. No need for Dad to hear how soppy I could be. "I love you a lot, Patchie Pie. You're my absolutely best friend, even more than Brian." Who actually wasn't even my friend anymore. But no need to tell Patch that. "Come on out, Patch." I rattled the dish again. "This is yummy. I might eat it myself if you don't come fast."

Not a sound except for a car whizzing past on the road and an airplane droning above us.

"Patch! Patch!"

It was then I saw that the gate I'd closed behind Dad was open. And I knew Patch was gone.

Chapter 8

Mom turned off the stove, and she and Dad and I dashed out to the car, not even stopping to lock the doors. We drove slowly with all the windows down, Mom and I sticking our heads out and calling, "Patch! Patch!" every few seconds. My heart was doing a hollow thumping like a toy drum. It thumped even more when Mom yelled to Dad, "Stop! Stop! There are posters on some of these lampposts. Maybe somebody has already found him." She clasped her hands and closed her eyes. "Oh, wouldn't that be the best thing ever?"

"It's too soon, honey," Dad said. "Don't get your hopes up."

"And those posters have been there for a while," I said. "Somebody else has lost something. I've seen them."

"Oh." Mom's sigh was defeated. I prayed she wouldn't ask who or what. But she was too worried about Patchie to be curious.

I crouched in the backseat by the open window feeling sick. Patchie missing, Mouser missing for Sally. And all of it my fault.

"The thing is," Mom said, "I don't know if Patch is smart about traffic. He's always on a leash when he's out. He's so smart about other things, but . . ." She sounded frantic. Then I saw her realize that I was sitting in back, and scared out of my wits, too, and she turned and patted my knee and said in a fake cheerful voice, "I'm just having a nervous negative reaction. We'll find him."

I hardly noticed where we were as we drove along the silent lamp-lit streets, all the houses with happy lights on their porches, the sounds of television news, of music, coming through open windows. All I could think of was finding the big white dog with the black patch over one eye. And then I realized we were on Craig, cruising past 365. I looked fast and saw that there was nothing hanging on the tree. I glanced back through the rear window. The corner of the envelope I'd left sticking out of the mailbox was gone. Which meant someone had taken my note inside. All of that seemed somehow far away, as if it had happened a long time ago to somebody else.

"Dad! Quick! Turn here," I said. "I bet Patchie went to Brian's. He likes Brian even though he hates Jehosephat."

Suddenly I was excited.

I ran up the path to Brian's house, almost before Dad stopped the car, and leaned on the bell. Looking back, I realized our car was parked right under the lamppost with the mouse notice. But it was so directly under it, Mom and Dad wouldn't see it unless they got out. Maybe it would be better if they did see it. I was sick of all this scheming and lying, though I'd been careful not to totally lie. I'd half lied. Or maybe I just hadn't told all the truth, which was probably just as bad.

When Brian opened the door, he scowled at me. "What's up?"

I'd forgotten we weren't friends

anymore. But when I told him Patch had run away, he stopped scowling.

"How come?" he asked.

I shrugged. "He just did."

"Hey! I know why," Brian began, then glanced around as his mom appeared.

"You've lost Patch?" she asked. "Oh no. Why don't you both go check the backyard?"

She went out to talk to Mom and Dad, and Brian and I ran to the back, calling Patch's name.

There was no answer.

"Maybe he went to Grant Park," Brian suggested. "We've played ball with him there a bunch of times."

I nodded. "Yeah. Good idea."

"I'll come help you search if you like," Brian said, and his mom said that would be O.K.

At Grant Park we got out of the car and searched among the swings and slides, so still and quiet.

"You know exactly why he ran away, don't you?" Brian asked when we were a little distance from Mom and Dad.

"Because of me," I said. "I've messed up a lot of things. I made this big fuss over Reggie and ignored him. He thought I didn't like him anymore."

"Yeah, yeah, yeah," Brian agreed. "It's Patch you should be telling that to, not me."

"You're such a know-it-all," I said. "As if you never made a mistake."

"Well, what are you going to do about Reggie now?"

"Oh." I tried to sound vague. "You don't know what's happened. I've bought him."

Brian stopped, peering at me in the near dark. "Bought him?" he repeated.

"Sh! Here's Dad. Chop, chop," I warned, hitting my inside elbow with the side of my hand.

Dad said they'd decided they should take Mom home in case Patch came back, and she'd call the Humane Society, because someone might have found him and he'd be there, in the pound, just waiting for us to go pick him up.

We took Brian home first. "Good luck," he called. I thought maybe our non-friendship was over, kind of.

The Humane Society was such a good idea that we didn't wait to get back to our house. Mom called them on the cell phone. But they said no white dog with a black patch had been brought in tonight or today.

"But you know what they asked me?" Mom told us when she rang off. "They asked if he had a nametag on his collar, and I told them of course, and they said it was likely someone would call us. In all the worry, I completely forgot our phone number is right there, hanging around his neck. Thank goodness." She sounded almost cheerful. "We'll get him back."

"But what if whoever finds him decides to keep him?" I whispered. "He's a really cute dog."

Mom shook her head. "No one would be mean enough to do that."

"Somebody might," I said. And I was sorry, sorry, sorry I'd been mean enough to keep Reggie mouse.

Chapter 9

**W**e had no call from a finder when we got home.

Dad and I cruised the streets again. No Patch.

Back in the kitchen we didn't mention the meatballs, cold in the pan. There were scummy islands floating on top of the pasta water. I saw Australia. And a long skinny water snake with two heads.

Mom made hot chocolate, and Dad fixed toast. I held Reggie, and the feel of him in my hand made me want to cry.

The dog dish with the kibble sat on the floor by the dishwasher.

"Kibbles 'n Bits, Kibbles 'n Bits," I'd tease, holding the bowl just out of Patch's reach, and he'd jump up and snap at it, but gently because he knew it was just a game. I definitely needed to cry.

"Patchie must be hungry," I said, blinking hard. "If he was home, I'd fix him a big huge dinner of all the things he likes best—pizza and peanut butter and sardines and meat loaf . . . and oatmeal cookies." I was blinking fast, but still everything was blurred.

Mom laughed a bogus laugh. "Whoa there! We don't want to make him sick the minute we get him back."

The phone rang twice, and we rushed at it. The first time was Aunt Sophie, the second time was Brian.

"Did he come home yet?" Brian asked.

"Uh-uh. And I can't talk. We have to keep the line free."

Yesterday little Sally had probably been hanging about, waiting and hoping for a phone call. Had she made a decision yet? Definitely she'd read my note by now. Or Ira or her mom had read it to her. Suppose someone came by and offered me $47.35 so they could keep Patchie? I'd never say yes. Not if they gave me fifteen hundred dollars. Not for all the money in the world. Why did I ever think Sally would take cash for Reggie?

"I think it's time for bed," Mom said gently.

I didn't argue.

I put Reggie beside me on the pillow, my fingers curled around him. But there was no dog weight on my feet, no soft snores or tumble turns as

Patch made himself comfortable. No warm dog trying to sneak under my covers.

I held Reggie tightly in my hand.

"I want to keep you," I sniffled. "But you know what?" I pushed my face against my pillow. "You're not Pony Boy and you're not mine. So I don't think you'll ever really belong to me. Maybe I can come visit you?

Will that be good? Maybe I won't feel so bad when Patchie comes back."

Once I woke up in the night and thought I heard my dog scratching at the back door. I rushed downstairs. But I'd dreamed it, or imagined it. It was only a tree branch scraping against the window.

I got up early while it was still almost dark.

The house was sleeping.

I checked outside for Patch, but there was no Patchie.

I went back upstairs then and put Reggie in the little box and curled his tail neatly around him. He looked up at me with his black button eyes, and I decided he understood how hard this was for me. I sniffed, whispered, "Good-bye, Mouser," and put the lid on.

My bike made no sound as I rode down our street. But dogs sensed I was there and barked their heads off. None of those barks belonged to Patchie. The streetlights glowed faintly, and there was still a sprinkle of stars in the sky, so faint I could hardly see them.

Here was 365 Craig. And oh my gosh! I stopped fast and dropped my bike in the grass. Something hung from the tree, something on a broad ribbon. I clutched Reggie's box hard. Sally was going to take the money after all. My heart flipped and flopped. If she did, then Reggie would be mine.

I tiptoed over the grass. It was wet and long and soaked my sneakers with early morning dew. I smelled roses. Pinned to the ribbon was a note and something else. My fingers were fat and useless as I struggled to untie the knot. The note was hard to read. I held it up toward the gleam from the street lamp. GIVE ME BACK MY MOUSER, it said. Pinned to it was an envelope that I recognized. Inside was my $47.35.

I glanced up at the windows of the house. All the miniblinds were closed tight. No one watching.

I set the box on the front step, under the porch roof, and put my envelope underneath it. Sally should have the money, too, because of how sad I'd made her. That would only be fair. I stood for a minute or two, looking at that envelope, and then I decided it would be O.K. to give her only half. After all, she did get her mouse back, and she'd actually only had one day of pain and suffering. Forty-seven bucks was a lot of money. I was sure half would buy a really awesome tiara. I took two ten-dollar bills and stuffed them in my pocket.

I tiptoed again across the grass. Wait, wait! I chewed on my lip for a

while, went back, opened the envelope, and shoved the twenty dollars
back inside. Pain and suffering even
for a day wasn't fun. I knew.

I pushed my bike for half a block
so they wouldn't hear me beating my
retreat. Then I jammed for home.

Chapter 10

Mom was fixing oatmeal. She looked up as I came in. "Have you been out already, searching for Patchie?" Her voice was soft.

"I did look for him," I said. "But . . ." I watched her spoon oatmeal into a bowl for me and into one for herself. She sprinkled fat raisins on top. Did I really need to say anything more? But I did need to. "I went to take Reggie back to the little girl who owned him," I muttered, turning my back to Mom and washing my hands at the kitchen sink, half hoping she wouldn't hear.

All was silent behind me.

"Her name is Sally," I said and made myself look around.

Mom was staring at me. "But how did you find her?"

"I read her address. On those posters."

"Oh, honey! That was hard for you to give up the little mouse. Really hard."

I sat at the table and poured milk from the pitcher into the oatmeal and waited for her to make the connection. Posters. Reggie. There were two heartbeats of quiet. Then Mom said in a tight kind of way, "When did you find out who owned him?"

Here it came. It was hard to look up at her, but I did.

"Almost as soon as I found him," I said.

"Oh, Alex!"

I tried a shrug. "I wanted to keep him."

Fortunately, Dad came in the kitchen just then. "No time for breakfast," he said, grabbing a banana. "I'm already late. Any news about Patch?"

"Nothing," Mom said.

"I'm going to make posters today and put them up," I told him.

"Posters can work," Mom added with a sideways glance at me. "Alex might tell you all about how well posters work when you get home tonight."

Oh brother! I thought. Something else to look forward to. And then I thought . . . serves me right!

We made the posters and stuck them beneath the mouse posters, which were still there.

"What is it this time?" Mrs. Escondito asked as we walked past her house. She was out watering her roses, as usual. Watering the roses in your front yard is probably a good thing to do if you're nosy and want to know everything that's going on.

"We've lost our dog, Patch," I said. "White with a black patch over this eye." I cupped my hand over my right eye to demonstrate. "Have you seen him?"

She shook her head. "This street's getting to be like some sort of public billboard," she grumbled. "You'll be advertising the end-of-summer sales next."

"I don't think so," Mom said pleasantly. "Your roses are lovely."

"It's all that water," I muttered.

"I hope you find your dog," Mrs. Escondito called after us.

"Thanks," I called back.

Mom and I hung out at home all day, hoping for a phone call. There were lots, but none about Patch. We tried the Humane Society again.

Brian came over, and he and I shot a few baskets and played a few video games. We're reading the same Harry Potter book, and we lay head to toe on my bed and discussed whether or not we could actually be wizards ourselves and not know it.

I couldn't concentrate.

Had someone found Patch and not called in? Or was he lost somewhere, exhausted and scared, trying to find his way home? It hurt so much to imagine him, but I couldn't stop.

Downstairs, Liberace was trilling his fingers across the piano keys. It sounded like someone running a stick along a railing, only more musical.

I'd told Brian all about the return of Sally's mouse.

"He sure was cool," Brian said. "But you keeping him wasn't."

"I know. I know."

Brian rubbed his arms. "Is the sacred promise canceled?"

"Yeah. But still, don't go blabbing around what I did."

"Did you ever notice, when you're under the sacred promise your arms ache, even if you haven't told?" Brian asked. "It's as if they're preparing themselves for the big chop."

"It's called phantom pain. Or ghost pain," I explained. "It can happen when a person has his legs cut off. By a doctor, I mean. In an operation, maybe to save his life or something. He can still feel them. They itch, and there's nothing there to scratch."

Brian sat up on the bed. "Wow! That would be bad. How do you know all these things, anyway?"

"My mom," I said. "She researches."

I went across to my window again, still looking for Patch. I kept thinking that I'd do that one time, and he'd be walking along the street, calmly strolling home.

"Patchie! Patchie!" I whispered and put my face close to the glass. But the street and the sidewalk were empty.

Chapter 11

Brian and I were out shooting baskets in the driveway the next day when Ira came by. "Wanna play?" I asked.

"Sure." He came through our gate, which we were leaving open now so Patchie could get in, day or night. Not that he couldn't open the gate. We knew he could. But we wanted to make it easy for him.

"Too bad about your dog," Ira said. "I saw your posters when I was taking ours down. Sally got her mouse back." He rolled his eyes. "Whoever took it left her 47 bucks, too. I don't know why. Last night Mom had to drive us, plus Mouser, to the party shop so Sally could buy her tiara. It cost ten bucks, so she has 37 dollars left. She's strutting around the house being the rich fairy princess of the world."

"Cool," I muttered, bouncing the basketball against my knee and thinking that I definitely should have kept half of that money when I had the chance.

"I guess whoever took Mouser had this humongous guilty conscience," Ira said.

"Yeah. And was an O.K. guy," Brian said quickly without looking at me.

I gave him a grateful glance.

It did seem, though, that since I'd been honest, the laws of karma should now let me get Patchie back.

Karma means when you do something good, good is supposed to come down on you. I'm not sure if it always works. I missed Patch so much. And I missed Reggie, too. I kept getting him mixed up in my head with Pony Boy, and last night I dreamed that I was looking over the railing of a ship and there was Reggie floating away below me on the bright blue water.

But in my dream I waved to him and I wasn't that sad.

Time passed and passed.

We had two false alarms that turned out to be the wrong dog.

There was rain, and a lot of our posters lay plastered to the sidewalk. Our hopes were not bright anymore, either.

One day I noticed that Patch's food dish had been put away and that his two favorite rubber bones had disappeared. It seemed too final. I wandered out to the yard and I found the old chewed-up sneaker still there, which comforted me a lot.

It was getting to be the end of summer vacation.

I came in the kitchen one afternoon, and Mom was sitting at the table preparing her lessons for the new school year. I realized I hadn't heard her play the piano for a long time. I got myself a chocolate chip cookie out of the tin and leaned against the counter, munching.

"Do you know why chocolate chips stay the same shape even when you bake them in a hot oven?" Mom asked me, doing her thing.

"I have no idea," I said.

"They're baked at 350 degrees,

which is way above the melting point of chocolate, so you'd think they'd smear all over the place, wouldn't you?" Mom was warming to her subject, I told myself, pleased with my joke.

"Well, at the same time the chocolate melts, the cookie dough hardens, and it's too solid for the chocolate to ooze through, so the chips are trapped." She snapped her fingers. "Voilà!"

Voilà means "that's it" in French. Mom likes to pass some French words by me now and again.

"I was thinking I might get my class . . . ," she began, and stopped.

There was a scratching at the door.

Mom put her hands across her mouth, and her eyes widened.

"Patchie!" I shouted and I ran, slipping and sliding across the

kitchen floor to fling the door open.
And there on the step was Patchie,
his head cocked to one side, his
tongue lolling. It was as if, plain as
anything, he was saying, "I'm home."

I threw myself on him and wrapped my arms around his neck, and Mom came running and knelt down and wrapped her arms around his belly, and we were squeezing and hugging and kissing his head and face. He smelled ultra doggy.

"That's not his collar," Mom said, sniffling and fishing a tissue from the pocket of her jeans. "Oh, Patchie, somebody found you and kept you, but you got out and made it home. I always said you were as good as Houdini."

"Here boy, here boy!" I backed into the kitchen, and he followed, not frolicking or jumping on me, but wagging his tail.

"He's tired," Mom said. "I think he's come a long way."

We got out his nice clean dish,

and Mom found the bag of kibble in the back of the cupboard. "It's been here, waiting for you," she told him.

I didn't offer him all those things I'd thought of giving him, the sardines and the peanut butter and all that stuff, because I sure didn't want him to be sick. But I sat on the floor beside him as he ate, and he kept pausing to smile up at me. Patch never pauses when he's eating, but he knew this was special.

When Dad came home, we tried to figure out exactly what had happened. "His collar with his tag could have come off somehow, if he scraped under a fence or a gate," Dad said.

"We never kept it tight," I added.

"He's been well cared for." Dad smoothed his hand along Patchie's back. "Somebody liked you enough to keep you. They liked you too much to try to find your real owner."

I kept my head down.

We decided not to bother Patch with a bath that night, even though he smelled like fish manure, if there's any such thing. But Mom said he could sleep with me as usual, and tomorrow we'd bathe him, and me, and wash the bedclothes, too. She said Patch didn't need any water worries until he'd had a good night's sleep.

So he lay, warm across my feet the way he always did, turning and tumbling until he got comfortable and then sneaking up right under my covers. Maybe Mouser was sleeping tonight with little Sally. Did she wear her tiara to bed?

I was almost asleep, holding Patchie's paw, when I heard Mom playing the piano downstairs. "Für Elise"!

Way to go, Mom, I thought.

"She's just about as good as Mozart," I told Patch, and I lay there, smiling, happy enough to burst.